SHONEN JUMP'S
Yu-Gi-Oh! GX™

Adapted by Tracey West

JADEN'S SECRET

SCHOLASTIC INC.

New York   Toronto   London   Auckland   Sydney
Mexico City   New Delhi   Hong Kong   Buenos Aires

ISBN 0-439-88838-7

©1996 Kazuki Takahashi
©2004 NAS•TV TOKYO

Published by Scholastic Inc.
SCHOLASTIC and associated logos are trademarks and/or registered trademarks of Scholastic Inc.

12 11 10 9 8 7 6 5 4 3 2 1   6 7 8 9 10 11/0

Printed in the U.S.A.
First printing, September 2006

Jaden Yuki ran across Academy Island.
He had two big tests to take today. But he was late!

On the way, he saw a woman pushing her car up the hill. Jaden knew he wouldn't be on time if stopped to help. But he was never on time anyway!

"Never fear, Jaden's here!" he said.

Jaden got to his written test late.

He and his friend Syrus slept through most of it.

"You two might want to wake up," said Bastion, one of the top students at the academy. "The new rare cards arrived today."

"Let's go!" Jaden cried.

Jaden and Syrus ran to the card shack.
But there were no cards left!
"I'm done for!" Syrus wailed. "Now I'm
going to flunk my duel test!"

But the woman at the card shack recognized Jaden.

"I have something for you," she said. "Just call it a thank you for helping me with my car."

Across campus, a teacher named Dr. Crowler talked to Chazz, a student. They both wanted to see Jaden defeated.

Dr. Crowler told Chazz that he would fix the test so Chazz could battle Jaden!

"And you can use these rare cards to beat him!" he said.

Jaden and Syrus went to the dueling arena to take their tests. Jaden was shocked that he would be battling Chazz.

"That's right!" Dr. Crowler said. "I pulled some strings to make sure you got the challenge you deserve."

Jaden and Chazz faced off on the dueling field.

They charged up their Duel Disks.

"Duel!" the two boys called out.

Jaden made the first move. "I play Elemental Hero Clayman in defense!" he said.

"That oversized pile of pebbles doesn't have a chance against me," Chazz laughed.

Chazz played V-Tiger Jet!
Then he used Frontline Base.
"This card lets me summon another
level 4 monster," Chazz said.

Chazz played W-Wing Catapult in attack mode.

Then he merged the two cards.

"All right—the VW-Tiger Catapult!" Chazz cried.

Chazz had one more move. "With Tiger Catapult, I can force one of your monsters into attack mode," he said.

Jaden frowned. That left him defenseless!

VW-Tiger Catapult blasted Clayman with Heatseeker Blitz!

Clayman vanished from the field.

Jaden's life points dropped.

But Jaden did not look worried.
"I'm just getting warmed up!" he cried.
"I call Elemental Hero Sparkman in
defense mode."

Then he threw down a facedown.

Syrus and Bastion watched from the stands.

"There's not much else he can do with all of those rare cards Chazz seems to have," Bastion said.

"It's just not fair!" Syrus said.

But Chazz was just getting started.

"Ready for round two?" he cried. "Well, X-Head Cannon is! And, thanks to Front-line's magic, so is Z-Metal Tank as well!"

Then he used Call of the Haunted to bring back Y Dragon Head.

Y Dragon Head joined with the other two monsters to create XYZ Dragon Cannon.

Then it joined with VW-Tiger Catapult to form V to Z Dragon Catapult Cannon!

The mega robot had a special ability. Chazz took Jaden's Sparkman off of the field.

But Jaden had a plan.

"I have a trap!" he cried. "A Hero Emerges!"

Chazz had to pick a card from Jaden's hand.

It was Elemental Hero Burstinatrix.

Chazz laughed. "That's okay. When Dragon Catapult Cannon attacks, I get to choose your monster's mode. And you know what? I choose attack mode!"

Jaden groaned. Once more, he had no defenses.

V to Z Dragon Catapult Cannon blasted Burstinatrix.

Jaden's life points dropped to 1000.

But Jaden was not worried. Chazz
was not the only one with rare cards.
The woman at the card shack had given
Jaden some, too.

First Jaden called an old friend.

"I summon Winged Kuriboh in defense!"

The cute little monster came onto the field.

"And I'll throw a facedown, too," Jaden said.

"Ha!" Chazz cried. "There's about to be a fried furball on the field!"

A white hot light burst from Chazz's monster.

But Jaden just smiled. "Secret weapon time!" he cried. "I sacrifice two cards and activate Transcended Wings!"

In the stands, everyone gasped at the sight of the rare card.

"Where did he get that?" Dr. Crowler fumed.

"Transcended Wings evolves Winged Kuriboh into a level 10 monster!" Jaden cried.

Kuriboh changed into a huge creature. It sent the attack right back to V to Z Dragon Catapult Cannon. *Bam!* The monster exploded Chazz's life points dropped to 1000.

"Elemental Hero Avian!" Jaden cried.
"Attack!"

The winged hero flew toward Chazz.

Chazz had no defenses. He lost all of
his life points.

The crowd cheered.

"Jaden did it!" Syrus yelled.

Only Dr. Crowler was not happy.

"Well played, Jaden," said the school headmaster. "It is with great pride that I promote you to Ra Yellow."

Everyone cheered. But Syrus was sad.

"Hopefully we can still be friends," he said.

But Jaden wasn't going anywhere!
"Sure, Ra Yellow is nice," he said. "But without you, Syrus, it's just not my home."